Clara J. Armstrong

La Porte in June

Clara J. Armstrong

La Porte in June

ISBN/EAN: 9783337156305

Printed in Europe, USA, Canada, Australia, Japan

Cover: Foto ©Andreas Hilbeck / pixelio.de

More available books at **www.hansebooks.com**

LA PORTE IN JUNE

BY
CLARA J. ARMSTRONG

CHICAGO
R. R. DONNELLEY & SONS COMPANY
1899

TO THE PEOPLE OF LA PORTE,
AMONGST WHOM I HAVE LIVED CONTENTEDLY
ALL MY LIFE,
THIS LITTLE BOOK IS RESPECTFULLY
DEDICATED.

Many years have elapsed since the first poem herein was written, and materially La Porte has changed. She has extended her boundaries in every direction, and has become more populous. The "one long street" for trade has now several branches, and room has been made at different points for various thriving industries. But the spirit of peace still nestles in the shade of her streets and long avenues, and she still retains that quiet, restful atmosphere which makes her distinctively a City of Sweet Homes.

LA PORTE IN JUNE

A city lapped on a fruitful plain,
Bright clover meadows and fields of grain
Wave around it, and send their sweets
To the cottage doors in the quiet streets.
There are miles of heavenly blue on high,
And miles of the richest emerald dye,
Spread on the teeming earth below.
Far as the dazzled sight can go,
Save to the north, where the green line breaks
For the crystal flash of lovely lakes ;
A jewel chain on the prairie's breast,
That shines and trembles in bright unrest ;

As the happy earth swings day and night
Out of the shadow into the light,
Sings, as it swings to a joyful tune,
Into the golden light of June.

June, in the beautiful bowery town
Where the level streets stretch smoothly down
Through lines of maple and oak and pine,
Garnished by many a graceful vine.
There is one long street for traffic and trade—
All the others for peace and shade ;
And nestlike homes, row after row,
With walls of garnet and brown and snow,
Veiled by the shadows of trees and bowers
Of evergreen shrubs and fragrant flowers ;
From lowly cottage to lofty hall
Leafage and bloom adorn them all.
Where in the wide West will you meet
Such sylvan charms in a city street—
Such wealth of blossoms and grand old trees ;
Such mingled music of birds and breeze ?
Surely the human life must be
Better for such sweet company.
Behold the fountains sparkling fair,
Cooling the languid summer air
With gentle showers of dewy spray,
Rising and falling the livelong day;

Rising and falling in silvery drips
Soft as the kisses from baby lips.
The eglantine at the window-sill
Shakes to the caged canary's trill ;

And the children pause in their evening play
To hear the oriole's wilder lay
Float down from the top of a tall oak tree
Glad as a free bird's song can be.
Here is a cool and calm retreat
For the weary soul and the wandering feet ;
No sweet homes on earth more sweet.

Come in the quiet afternoon
And set your spirit's harp in tune
With Nature's joyous pulse that plays
In all her thousand mystic ways ;
And garner up while June is here
Souls full of summer for the year.
Take from the lily's golden heart
Unto thine own a spotless part.
Take from the rose her fragrant breath,
And cherish it for life and death.
Of health and joy, a generous share,
Take from the bounteous, blessed air ;
Then freely give—as the earth gives sheaves,
And prairie grasses, and forest leaves—
When winter storms around you roll
Give forth the summer of the soul.

*   *   *   *   *

The lakes are still as lakes of glass,
The shadowy clouds above them pass ;
The earth and heaven almost seem
Like the figures in a mixed dream,
Reflected in the wave below;
Which is the real—you hardly know—
Upon the pictured glassy tide ?
Behold that fairy steamer ride,
Like a graceful bird upon the wing,
Or a little maiden in a swing ;

She floats so light, she glides so free,
Over the fairy land-locked sea.
Her colors fly out far and gay,
She wears a festal fine array,

And bears her merry crew along
With many a laugh and many a song,
To seek some haven of repose
From all their little cares and woes.

And may they find it—winter's gloom
Treads close upon the summer's bloom;

And care, when it abides too long,
Will sear the heart however strong.
Soon may they find it—ere the day
Has fled forever, on its way
To stand afar on Time's dim shore
With ghosts of those lost long before ;
Which slipped away ere yet we knew
That days in June are all too few.

THE BUILDING OF THE SPIRE

JULY, 1884

How long the cedar and the pine
   In nature's patient hand must wait
   Before they reach their full estate
As perfect columns in her shrine.

But man, with a magician's power,
   Seizes what all the years have wrought,
   And shapes it to his deepest thought
In the brief circle of his hour.

From my high window in the west
  I watched the building of the spire,
  As dark against the sunset's fire
It towered above the grove's green crest.

I heard the ringing hammers play
  In hands unfaltering, strong, and true,
  While firmly up toward the blue
The builders mounted day by day.

When suddenly complete and fair
  In the tall pinnacle's strong hold
  The golden ball and cross of gold
Rose, shining in the summer air.

Will it not vanish like a dream,
  Or pass with sunset's crimson cloud,
  Or with the morning's misty shroud
Melt in Aurora's earliest beam ?

Ah, no ; firm as the oak it stands ;
  The sun shall greet it many a year ;
  And one by one will disappear
The builders with the busy hands.

Yet still above the grove's green crest
  The " Kyrkan's " lofty spire will rise
  To meet the gaze of other eyes
From my high window in the west.

14

When the tired traveler from afar
   Beholds the spire whose shadow falls
   Beside his own dear cottage walls
Under the blessed evening star,

That slender signal in the sky,
   Straight as the needle to the pole
   Marks the bright magnets of his soul,
The home on earth—the Home on high.

THE OLD BOOK

My treasured book, my poet's soul,
　　Since first I marked you for my own
The years have called a lengthy roll,
　　And worn and gray we both have grown.
Your tarnished gold, my failing eyes,
　　Bear witness to the hand of time.
I feel it with a sad surprise
　　We have outlived our youthful prime.

But what are surface stains to you,
　　Who speak from every faded page
The thought forever young and true,
　　The visions all untouched by age ?
Between these covers worn and old
　　A wondrous realm of beauty lies ;
Where Life and Love and Death unfold
　　To music from the upper skies.

Sir Galahad and sweet Elaine,
　　And the " fair women" of the " Dream,"
King Arthur and his courtly train,
　　Bright spirits all to me they seem

Here first I met them ; here first fell
    The deep-toned "voices" on my ear,
And that grand dirge whose solemn knell
    Thrilled round the world from Hallam's bier.

When dark and dreary was the day,
    And sullen clouds did overbend
Beyond " the hills and far away,"
    I slipped with this dear poet friend.
I lingered oft in " Lotus Land,"
    And oft in Arden's lonely isle,
Or, when the Princess waved her hand,
    Breathed her enchanted air awhile.

I heard the " horns of Elfland blow";
    I heard a sweet song's dying fall,
And saw beyond the sunset's glow
    The " splendor on the castle wall."
In her still bower beside the stream
    I found the " Lady of Shalott"—
On earth and sky beheld " The Gleam,"
    And sordid cares were all forgot.

Oh, Poet of the magic power,
    Who sat upon the mountain height
Chanting your dreams from hour to hour,
    While the world listened with delight—

17

You sway our souls unto your law
    Of melody and beauty wrought,
And up to clearer levels draw
    The turbid stream of common thought!

THE JUBILEE YEAR—1876

The storm-clouds are brooding aloft in the
    air,
  And the clarion blast whistles loud at the
    door,
While the shadow of fear and the phantom of
    care
  Enter in where they never had entered
    before.

Oh, Jubilee Year! the first notes of thy song
  Are minor-keyed melodies, sad to the
    soul,
For the strong men have given their strength
    to the wrong,
  And dishonored their names on the National
    Scroll.

The working-man sits with his idle arms
    crossed
  By the want-stricken hearth, with a sigh in
    his breast,

For the Spring is at hand, but the Winter was
    lost ;
  He had rest, but no comfort nor joy in his
    rest.
Oh, Jubilee Year ! ere thy blossoms have come
  And March winds are tempered by perfumes
    of May,
Hear the laborer's prayer ; let the busy earth
    hum
  To the grand hymn of Industry, day after
    day !

The Century roundeth to fullness ; the flower,
  Whose beauty the whole world is longing
    to see,
Should look on a people, the wealth of whose
    power
  Is in freedom to learn what it means to be
    free.

Free to live, free to love, and work as men
    should,
  As true brothers and friends in the work-
    shop of God.
To work wisely for self, and the great common
    good,
  For the eyes of the nations who watch from
    abroad.

Oh, Jubilee Year! the first notes of thy song
  Are minor-keyed melodies sad to the soul.
Oh, grant us the last chords triumphant and
    strong!
  Give us honest men's names on the National
    Scroll.

CARVED ON A STONE

There was a light, which shone from tender
    eyes,
  A melody that rang from tuneful lips ;
  They vanished—like a star that trembling
    slips
Out of the autumn skies.

And gently here, beneath this marble stone,
  Life's broken harp was gathered to the rest
  Which nature giveth to the empty breast ;
The chrysalis outgrown.

We thought she seemed like a fair rose in June,
  She wore such royal colors in her face ;
  A lovely flower who made a fragrant place,
And dropped her leaves too soon.

But in the garden where she used to grow
  There lingers yet, and will forevermore,
  A something sweet which was not there
    before,
Though roses always blow.

And evermore the echo of a song—
"Remember me" — sighs near the garden
walls,
As with a strain of music swells and falls
A young voice clear and strong.

She liveth still, not to the grosser sense ;
We dwell so far below the spirit spheres ;
But love will keep through all the changing
years
Love's finer elements.

And sometimes in a pause of life's unrest
Some holy hush of twilight and repose,
The shadows wav'ring break — and then
disclose
A bright face heaven-blest.

No word is spoken—soul to soul is known—
And soul to soul diviner meanings teach
Than ever clothed themselves in mortal
speech
To be carved on a stone.

THE FASHIONS FOR MAY

Madame Nature is making the yearly display
Of her latest designs in her old winning
way.
Her soft emerald veil floating out on the
breeze
Has been caught on the heads of the skeleton
trees—
All her colors are blended with consummate
skill,
And her draperies trail o'er the plain and the
hill
With the generous sweep of a prodigal queen ;
Grass-fringed and leaf-broidered in velvety
green.
What sweet flowers she wears ? What a mu-
sical throng
Make the gay bowers ring with its burden of
song !
And I thought as I listened I heard a bird
say,
" O to bloom and be fair is the fashion for
May !"

The dear Madame changes her modes with
    good reason ;
Her styles always suit with the times and the
    season ;
There is never a blossom or a bud out of place,
And her patterns are marvels of beauty and
    grace.
There are creeping pulsations in leaflet and
    root,
And the plan of the flower foreshadows the
    fruit.
There is work to be done ; there is growth to
    attain
From the slender young blade to the harvest
    of grain !

The woods must be trimmed and the roses
    unfolded,
The treasures of Autumn be painted and
    molded !
And no sound of the hammer or saw shall be
    heard,
For the planet rolls on to the song of the
    bird,
And silently draws from the depths of her
    bosom
The iron-limbed oak and the delicate blossom ;

And no man has learned how she works on
 the vine,
To bring out through its fibers her fountain of
 wine.
She giveth her nurslings their uses and graces,
And calleth from clouds and the far-distant
 spaces
The raindrops and secret electrical power
Which throbs in the heart of the rock and the
 flower ;
And to life's full fruition she leadeth the way
When adorning herself in the fashions for May.

Come, O daughters of Eve, let us read and be
 wise
In the great Book whose pages unfold to the
 skies !
For the fashions of May are the letters of light,
In which the Great Author of all loves to write ;
And " Life's manifestations," the text seems
 to say,
Are all good though in homely or lovely array;
But your souls seek for beauty, as bright waters
 run
To the sea ; as a flower lifts its face to the sun ;
You would float on the tide with a favoring
 breeze,

Or, like butterflies, bask in the sun at your ease ;
Forgetting how ceaseless and strong the en-
    deavor
Which Nature puts forth in the flower and
    river,
And always and ever the magical charm
Which the frosts cannot blight, nor the heat
    ever harm ;
Lies in spiritual growth, and the fashion of
    Truth,
Which outlive the gay fashions of beauty and
    youth :
Put your hands to some labor of love, and
    forget
That your brow has been sad and your eye-
    lashes wet ;
For the idle white fingers, so fair to the view,
Would be better for having some good work
    to do,
Still move on and move upward, grow grace-
    fully old,
And grow wiser and sweeter as years are
    unrolled ;
And though time swiftly glides, and your youth
    fades away,
You will wear in the spirit the fashion for May.

THE ROSE LOVER

Place no marble o'er his head,
But a red rose-tree instead !
Let white roses pale and sweet
Drop their blossoms round his feet !
Oft he went with willing hand,
Planting flowers about the land ;
Sowing in the desert spot
Heart'sease and forget-me-not ;
Leaving in his fragrant trail
Fairy lilies of the vale ;
But he ever loved the rose
More than any flower that grows.
Though the years were full of care,
Patiently he bore his share ;
While the rose sprang from the soil
He had courage for his toil.
Now the pilgrimage is done,
And the blessed goal is won,
Let the cover of his bed
With his favorite flower be spread.

SHADOW

The heart of the earth beats low to-night
Under her vestments of icy white ;
There is no music of pulse or breath,
The trance of winter is deep as death.
There is no music, but winds make moan,
And wander the dreary plains alone—
Sighing like mourners, who sigh and weep
By the grave-beds, where their lost loves sleep.
The stars have hidden their golden eyes,
In the cloudy veil that shrouds the skies,
And trails on the frozen waste below,
Its sable shadow across the snow.
Earth seems like a rudderless bark at sea,
To drift in the deep immensity,
To sink and to swoon from life and light,
Into the regions of Death and Night.

LIGHT

The planet keeps to her airy track,
In the star-gemmed ring of the Zodiac ;
Through blackest midnight, and gulfs of gloom
Where wild winds shriek like the voice of
       doom—
She rolls securely, and firm and fast,
Wheels into the sunward path at last.
Her life is constant—the Southlands glow
With verdure, beyond the lines of snow.
Though pale and cold to our Northern view,
She weareth a girdle of rainbow hue
Which under the deathless sun lies curled,
And broadens yearly around the world.
Ten thousand winters have failed to blight
Or quench the warmth of its living light ;
And never yet have the summers failed,
At the farthest point where ships have sailed,
To thrill, though with ever so light a hand,
The frozen life of the frozen land ;
To drop some blossom, however small,
By the Arctic sea and Alpine wall.

THE IRON WORKERS

Send a piercing iron note
From the engine's brazen throat !
Loose the belt and stop the wheel ;
Drop the tools of brass and steel ;
Shut the workshop, turn the key
Leave the still machinery.
Let its giant shadows fall,
Weird and silent on the wall,
Black against the moonbeams white ;
Till another workday's light.

Now for quiet, now for rest,
These of all things seem the best.
As a miser grasps his gold,
Do the iron forces hold
Firm resistance to our might,
In the long and stubborn fight ;
Every muscle strained and tense
Must make vigilant defense ;

Till our senses swim and reel,
Like the swift revolving wheel ;

Till our pulses throb and beat
Like the engine's in the heat ;
And to our own souls we seem
Men of iron, fire and steam.
So are earth's crude riches wrought ;
Into forms of human thought ;
Trade improves and commerce thrives,
While we battle for our lives.

Now for quiet, now for rest,
These of all things seem the best,
For tired limbs and weary brain,
Sleep will charm away the pain.
We may have a restful dream,
Of wild wood and gliding stream
From some breezy mountain side,
Drink of heaven's inflowing tide ;
From afar may catch the gleam
Of joys known only in a dream ;
For our higher natures crave,
From the cradle to the grave,
Something more 'twixt Life and Death,
Than the daily Bread and Breath.

Let earth a charmed silence keep
While we restful dream and sleep—
Sleep and dream of that blest age.
Long foretold by seer and sage,

When the working-man shall be
Heir of a nobler destiny,
Than for aye to delve and toil
In the grimy smoke and soil
With the burdens of the day
For the hireling's scanty pay,
With a starving, untaught soul
Chafing at the stern control
Of necessities that bind
Hand and foot and struggling mind,
Making all the rough ways straight,
That the world may ride in state,
While he walks with aching feet
Humbly to the grave's retreat.

That bright age shall find him still
Ready at the forge and mill,
With appliances of art
Which shall do the giant's part ;
And with Science at his side,
He will still direct and guide
All the elements of power
To the uses of the hour.
Still beneath the smiling skies
Mighty cities shall arise—
Banished deserts shall disclose
Gardens blooming like the rose—

Still his deeds of noble worth
Shall bless and beautify the earth.
But for him more leisure hours,
Less of iron, more of flowers ;
His life's music then shall be
Played upon a softer key.

He will sit at Wisdom's feet,
Learn to keep her counsel sweet.
He will find through visions high
Better ways to live and die—
Deepest problems solve anew
When the prophecies come true.

THE WHEELMAN

When the summer day is dewy and sweet—
  When the summer sun is but two hours
    high,
I can see from my cushioned window-seat
  A tall young man on his wheel go by.

As swift as a swallow he flashes past ;
  And onward, onward, forever on,
Must his watchword be, as he flies so fast
  Toward the rim of the distant horizon.

When the smoky breath of the restless town
  Mingles aloft with the breath of heaven,
He spins each morn o'er the long green down,
  And back with the birds to their nests at
    even.

He rides and he glides, and he treads the air,
  As if " Boundless Spaces " were all his
    own,
And he sits, well poised in his saddle there,
  As a king might sit on his gilded throne.

Oh, the joy of motion so fine and free,
  Of the swift pursuit of some prize afar,
Of sailing the buoyant, measureless sea
  Of air, by the touch of the handle-bar !

Oh, the wingéd words of old Homer's song,
  And the wingéd chargers that trod the sky !
How the ancient tales to my mem'ry throng
  When the tall, young man on his wheel
    goes by !

HER SMILE

My Dorothy Dimple, as old Time flies
He may dim the light of your brown, bright
      eyes,
He may fade the tints of your silken hair,
And wrinkle the cheek with the dimples fair,
And all that this robber of youth might do
I would not dare even to whisper you !

But Dorothy Dimple, never you mind,
He may bring you gifts of another kind,
For he is not truly a thief, you know,
But giving and taking, he makes one grow.

If you treat him kindly, and use him well,
You will fall but softly under his spell ;
And light will his touch be upon your brow,
If you smile in his face as you're smiling now.

TRUE FREEDOM

If the laboring man would be
Independent, strong, and free,
First, with all the foes within,
He the warfare must begin.
With envious low desires,
And with passion's baleful fires—
With the " weed " that numbs the brain,
And the " cup " that leaves a stain
On the lip, and on the life,
Let him wage a noble strife !
Victory will make him bold,
And his enemies of old—
Those who have oppressed him long—
Ignorance and Want and Wrong—
In his strengthened arm shall feel
Something keener far than steel !

THE MILLINER GIRL

You are sitting and stitching to-day
  'Midst a flutter of ribbons and lace,
Giving all the new bonnets for May
  Your own touch of the milliner's grace.
From the window you see the blue sky,
  And the clouds floating there in the sun,
And your bosom is stirred with a sigh,
  And a wish that the trimming was done.
But roses and ribbons are all in a whirl,
  And the ladies are waiting, my milliner girl.

O the maidens with black eyes and blue,
  And the matrons with dark locks and fair ;
They are watching and waiting for you,
  And the hats they are longing to wear ;
And 'tis little they heed how you sigh,
  Or how weary your fingers may be,
Each will say in her turn : " O do try
  To make something becoming to me."
For coil and for braid and for soft flowing curl
  Form a suitable setting, my milliner girl.

For these trifles that seem light as air
    Still are symbols of joy or of woe,
As they rest on the damsel's bright hair,
    Or the grandmother's light crown of snow;
For who would be garnished and gay
    When her heart and her fortunes are sad,
Or who, when the clouds pass away,
    Does not show by her hat she is glad.
Then a wreath for the bride, a plume and a
      pearl ;
    But crape for the mourner, my milliner girl.

And, dear milliner girl, as you sew,
    Take your stitches with womanly art,
And, while shaping the loop and the bow,
    May this thought bring a balm to your heart :
That the world needs you there in your place ;
    Needs the work which you only can do—
That the lilies have not so much grace
    As a maiden whose service is true—
In office or kitchen or there in the whirl
    Of your ribbons and roses, dear milliner girl.

THE DEMAND FOR TRUTH

Thus were we taught—that in Eden's bower
The serpent poisoned the fairest flower,
And planted the seed of a deathless sin
Which stealthily grew all hearts within;
And the ill he wrought had power to sever
Man from the face of his God forever.
The nations mourned the great disaster,
And strove to appease the avenging master;
But the wrath of God o'er his thwarted plan,
Still darkly followed his creature man,
In the raging seas, in the lightning's stroke
Which over the mountain in fury broke;
In the earthquake's shock, in the fiery rain
That the red volcano threw over the plain;
In the pestilent breath of a marshy fen,
And the jarring wars of the souls of men,
In every thorn on the earth's green sod
Was read a sign of the wrath of God.

But mixed with the ills which the serpent brought
There were grains of wisdom and gems of
        thought;

And the ages, bitter and slow and sweet,
Have ripened the harvest about our feet.
We face the future, and yet look back
Over the Old World's devious track ;
And searching the heart of the mighty past,
May ponder its lessons sad and vast.
We read by a glorious Light, whose ray
Has melted the wrath of the Lord away—
That shines on the Laws of the Universe,
All working in order, without the curse ;
And the struggling races of men, who climbed
As the plants climb sunward, and yet more
        blind
Than the vine—who knoweth its vital needs—
In their ignorant fear of kings and creeds,
But climbing and falling with laboring moan,
As slow as the continents, man has grown
Through woes unnumbered, through blood and
        tears,
From his childish faith and his slavish fears.

But climbing and falling and rising still
To a clearer brain, and a firmer will,
To a higher plane—to a keener sight,
To a larger heart—and a soul of might,
That has flung the shackles of fear away,
And is boldly asking for truth to-day.

For truth alone, though the heavens fall,
For man and for woman—the truth for all.
Though his cherished faith be swept away
Like the withered leaves of yesterday—
And though hope's fair structures be over-
       thrown,
He asks for truth, and the truth alone.
Then proffer not stones for bread, O ye
Who sit on the thrones of authority !
Nor jingle a counterfeit coin in view
Of a questioning world and call it true !
Lest the keen-eyed scorners of your deceit
Should rise and hurl you beneath their feet.